THE BABY-SITTERS CLUB

NOTEBOOK

SONIA BLACK AND PAT BRIGANDI

SCHOLASTIC INC.
New York Toronto London Auckland Sydney

Book design by Ira Hechtlinger.

ISBN 0-590-45074-3

12 11 10 9 8 7 6 5 4 3   1 2 3 4 5 6/9

Printed in the U.S.A.   40

INTRODUCTION

Got a question about baby-sitting? You're in luck! *Everything* you always wanted to know about the business of baby-sitting is right here in this book. Find out how to get and keep clients. Read about fun and games to help make your job much easier. Discover quick-and-easy snack recipes to prepare. Learn the do's and don'ts of good sitting, plus proper infant care, toddler care, and emergency care. There's also a list of recommended read-aloud books . . . and *lots* more. There's even plenty of space to jot down handy notes and reminders about each baby-sitting job.

So don't waste another minute. Start reading. If you practice the hot tips that are on these pages, your baby-sitting business will be booming before you know it!

READY . . . SET . . . GO!

With any new business, the hardest part is where to start. A good place to begin is to really **prepare** yourself for the job. First, read up on child care and baby-sitting. If your school or a local organization offers a special course in baby-sitting or child care, register if you can. Then practice your baby-sitting skills with a couple of free sittings.

Next, set up some **working guidelines** for yourself. Decide, for example, what days you'll be available for baby-sitting; what hours; what age children you'll be able to baby-sit; how many children at a time you think you can capably supervise; what rate of pay you expect for daytime sitting and for nighttime sitting.

The next step is to **spread the word.** Tell relatives, neighbors, teachers, and friends that you're available for baby-sitting jobs. Tell them your guidelines and expertise and ask them to pass the word to anyone they think may also need your services. You can even place an ad in your neighborhood newsletter. Or you can make up advertising flyers to hand out in the neighborhood. These flyers could also be posted (with permission) on bulletin boards or other attention-getting spots in such places as your local supermarket, laundromat, grocery store, church, school, or Y.

Your ad could read simply: Capable, reliable, dependable baby-sitter for hire. For further information call:

_____ at _____ .

    (your name)   (telephone number)

MEET 'N' GREET

Once you have a baby-sitting job lined up, it is a good idea to meet the parents and children before the day of the assignment. This way you won't be total strangers when you do arrive for the job.

Meeting the Parents. The important thing to remember about meeting parents is to **ask questions**. Find out as much as you can about the kids you will be sitting. Ask about the children's likes and dislikes: What food do they love; what food do they hate; what are their favorite TV shows; their favorite things to do, etc. Ask about what's off limits: Is there a particular room no one should enter? Is there a TV program the kids are not allowed to watch? Should you stay indoors, or is going outdoors permitted?

Find out what's expected of you — your specific **duties**. What sort of discipline do you administer if a child misbehaves? Ask where smoke alarms, fire extinguishers, or fire escapes are located. Ask if additional chores such as washing dishes, feeding pets, or watering plants are included with the assignment. Find out where the parents can be reached or who to call in case of an emergency while you're on the job. Make arrangements for how you will get home (especially if you're night sitting) when your job is over. Use the information pages in the back of this book to jot down all important facts.

Meeting the Kids. Be friendly but don't overwhelm the kids with *too much* friendliness. Don't try to be their best buddy in an instant. Don't be pushy. Introduce yourself by telling them your name and that you'll be baby-sitting them while their parents are away. Ask the kids their names and allow them to ask you any questions they might have about you. Then you can ask them questions about themselves. You can ask, for example, where they go to school, what grade they're in, their favorite subjects, their friends, toys, games, etc. The important thing to keep in mind is to make the kids feel at ease with you.

YOUR KID KIT

You can prepare a special "kid kit" to help you with your baby-sitting job. Here's a handy list to give you some ideas of things to pack in your kit:

playing cards
storybooks, comics
crayons and coloring books
board games
musical instruments (recorder, kazoo, harmonica, tin whistle, etc.)
camera
portable tape recorder
toys
balloons
writing paper and pencils
first aid kit

MORE STUFF . . .

Make up your own list of helpful items to take on the job.

☐ _____

☐ _____

☐ _____

☐ _____

☐ _____

☐ _____

☐ _____

☐ _____

☐ _____

☐ _____

☐ _____

☐ _____

☐ _____

☐ _____

☐ _____

DO'S AND DON'TS

Besides those already mentioned, there are other important do's and don'ts every good baby-sitter should practice. Check out the ones on the lists and add any others that you may think of.

Do's

Do arrive on time or even ten to fifteen minutes early for last-minute instructions from the parents.

Do dress appropriately. A good appearance is a plus.

Do make sure all entrances to the house are locked once the parents leave (more on page 28).

Do ask permission to make snacks for yourself, make telephone calls, use the stereo, etc.

Do give the kids your full attention.

Do tidy up any mess you've made or have the kids help you clean up any mess they've made.

Do make periodic checks on the kids while they're asleep.

☐ _____

☐ _____

☐ _____

Don'ts

Don't let anyone you don't know into the house (more on page 28).

Don't tell callers that you're alone with the kids — just take phone messages for the parents.

Don't stay on the telephone for long periods of time.

Don't spank the kids you're baby-sitting.

Don't play the stereo loudly.

Don't invite friends over.

Don't leave the kids alone in another room.

Don't argue with the kids.

Don't play dangerous games.

Don't snoop through personal belongings of your employer.

Don't fall asleep on the job.

☐ _____

☐ _____

☐ _____

☐ _____

☐ _____

☐ _____

☐ _____

☐ _____

WEE ONES

A baby-sitter has to use extra-special care when baby-sitting infants.

Sleepers. Though babies sleep a lot, they need special attention even when they are sleeping. Make periodic checks to see that the baby's pillow doesn't cover his face or that his blanket doesn't cover his head. Tuck blankets securely at the foot of the baby's crib.

Crying Time. Another thing that babies sometimes do a lot is cry. Generally babies cry when they need a **diaper change** or when they're **hungry**. When changing a diaper, make sure that you lay the infant on his back on a flat surface. Have all the necessary articles: baby powder, Vaseline, lotion, wet cloth, etc. close by. Never leave the child on a changing table where he or she could accidentally roll off to the floor. To prevent such accidents, you could even lay the infant on a blanket on the floor at changing time. When using cloth diapers, be very careful not to prick the baby's skin when you secure the diaper pins.

Feeding Time. Before the parents leave, find out if they have the baby's formula ready made or if you're expected to prepare the formula. If you are, get all the necessary instructions from the parents. Find out where the formula is kept, where the baby's bottles are kept, how much formula the baby should be given, when the baby should be fed. When you get ready to feed the baby, the formula should be lukewarm — never hot. To be sure the formula is just right, shake drops of it on the insides of your wrist or on the back of your hand. If you can hardly feel the liquid on your wrist, the temperature is just right. If the liquid feels hot, cool it down by running the bottle under cool tap water. If the liquid feels cold, stand the bottle in a panful of hot water for a few moments.

After feeding, **burp** the baby by resting his head on your shoulder and gently pat or rub his back. Remember, whenever you're holding the baby, *you must be sure to support his head and back at all times*.

A Special Reminder: When babies are crawling on the floor, be sure the floor is safe from any harmful objects such as pins, needles, staples, coins, etc. Any object smaller than the infant's mouth can be dangerous, even if it's not sharp or pointed. Babies love to put just about *anything* in their mouths.

PLAYTIME!

Infant Play. Babies also love to play. And when it comes to playtime, babies are very easy to please. To keep infants entertained, you can simply turn on their musical mobiles or music boxes, or pull out their toys. You can let them hold their stuffed animals, squeeze their squeeze toys, shake their rattles. Or you can sing them songs, read them stories, cuddle them, rock them, or just talk to them.

Older Youngsters. There are all sorts of fun activities to keep older kids entertained. The most important thing to remember when it comes to playtime is not to play any games in which the kids could harm themselves. Don't allow kids to play games that use sharp objects. Don't let kids jump from high places or lock one another in closets. Don't let them play games of see-how-much you can eat or drink, etc. If you do go outdoors to play, make sure kids are dressed appropriately — warmly for cold weather and coolly for warm or hot weather. And whatever you play, make sure the kids understand the rules of the game.

FUN 'N' GAMES!

Here's a long list of the fun games and activities for indoors and outdoors:

cards
board games
Frisbee
catch (with ball)
baseball
tag
pin the tail on the donkey
sack race
Simon says
red light, green light
coloring
hide 'n' seek
jump rope
tic-tac-toe
jacks
marbles
shadow making
clay play
singing songs

☐ _____

☐ _____

☐ _____

HA HA'S

Kids are always in the mood for laughs. And there's nothing like a bunch of good jokes to tickle their funny bones. Knock, knock jokes are especially terrific because the kids can participate. Here are a few to get the laughs started. You can have the kids help you make up others to add to the fun.

Knock, knock.
Who's there?
Dwayne.
Dwayne, who?
Dwayne the tub, I'm drowning!

Knock, knock.
Who's there?
Shelby.
Shelby, who?
Shelby comin' 'round the mountain when she comes!

Knock, knock
Who's there?
Eliza.
Eliza, who?
Eliza lot so don't believe him!

Knock, knock.
Who's there?
Yvonne.
Yvonne, who?
Yvonne to be alone!

Knock, knock.
Who's there?
Marylee.
Marylee, who?
Marylee we roll along, roll along . . . !

Knock, Knock.
Who's there?
Banana.
Banana, who?
Knock, knock.
Who's there?
Orange.
Orange, who?
Orange you glad I didn't say banana?

CREATIVE PLAY

A puppet show is perfect for quiet-time entertainment. You can use the kids' dolls or stuffed toys for puppets or make your own puppets. Ask the parents to give you an old sock and draw on a funny face with washable watercolor or colored chalk. You can even tape on cut-out paper eyes, nose, mouth, and hair. Put the sock over your hand and there you have it — a quick and easy puppet. Use your puppets to act out a familiar story or make up skits of your own.

For story ideas, here are a few old-time favorites you could use:

> The Three Little Pigs
> Goldilocks
> Sleeping Beauty
> Snow White
> Little Red Riding Hood

☐ _____

☐ _____

☐ _____

☐ _____

☐ _____

Story Game. While just *telling* stories to kids can be very enjoyable for them and for you, you can only double the fun if you turn storytelling into a game that you all make up as you go along. You may think of other variations, but here's one example.

You begin the story by saying, for instance, "Once upon a time there was a . . ." The next player continues the story from where you left off. But the players must pay close attention to what letter your last word ended on. That's because their first word must begin with the letter that comes after it in the alphabet. So the next player could say, for example, ". . . bad witch who lived in the woods . . ." The next player's first word has to begin with the letter "t." (Of course, you may give the kids as much help as needed. This way the game is not only fun but educational, too.) Where your string-along story ends is all up to you — and the kids!

READ-ALOUD MATERIAL

Here is a recommended list of books youngsters would enjoy:

For kids 3 to 5 years old:
Goodnight Moon by Margaret Wise Brown
Each Peach Pear Plum by Janet and Allan Ahlberg
Make Way for Ducklings by Robert McCloskey
Little Rabbit's Loose Tooth by Lucy Bate

For kids 5 to 8 years old:
Dr. DeSoto by William Steig
Fables by Arnold Lobel
Flat Stanley by Jeff Brown
Why Mosquitoes Buzz in Peoples' Ears by Verna Aardema

You can find these and many more books in your local bookstore or library.

"I'M HUNGRY!"

Often during a baby-sitting session you'll have to prepare a meal or a snack for the child and yourself. Here are some tasty treats that can't be beat:

Baked Cheese Sandwich

4 slices of cheese, American or Swiss
4 slices of bread
soft butter or margarine

- *Carefully heat the oven to 450°.*
- *Place 2 slices of cheese between 2 slices of bread.*
- *Spread the butter on the outsides of the sandwiches.*
- *Place the sandwiches on an ungreased cookie sheet and put the sheet into the oven.*
- *Bake the sandwiches for about 10 minutes or until the cheese melts and the bread is golden brown.*
- *This recipe makes two sandwiches.*

Tuna Treats

1 can (6½ ounces) of tuna
1 large dill pickle
¼ cup of mayonnaise or salad dressing
¼ teaspoon of lemon juice
8 slices of bread

- Drain the can of tuna and place the contents in a bowl.
- Chop the pickle into small pieces. Place it in the bowl with the tuna.
- Stir in the mayonnaise and lemon juice. Keep mixing until all of the tuna is covered with the mayonnaise.
- Spread 4 slices of bread with the tuna mix. Top with the remaining bread.
- Cut the sandwiches in half and serve.
- This recipe makes four sandwiches.

Peanutty Apple Snack

- Carefully cut out the core of an apple.
- Fill the center with a mixture of peanut butter and raisins.
- Cut the apple into sections and munch away.

"I'M THIRSTY!"

Of course, once you've given kids a bite to eat, they're going to have to have something to drink. Here are a few thirst-quenching suggestions:

Orange Juice Supreme

1 can (6 ounces) of frozen orange juice
1 cup of milk
2 cups of vanilla ice cream

- *Pour the frozen orange juice and the cup of milk into a blender.*
- *Scoop in the ice cream.*
- *Cover and carefully blend on high speed for a few seconds.*
- *Pour into a glass and drink!*
- *This makes three to four shakes.*

Chocolate Soda

1½ cups of milk
½ cup of chocolate syrup or instant cocoa
½ cup of club soda
4 scoops of chocolate ice cream

- *Put the milk, syrup and 2 scoops of ice cream into the blender and carefully mix well.*
- *Put 1 scoop of ice cream in each of two glasses.*

- *Pour the mixture into the glasses until they're ¾ full.*
- *Then pour in the club soda.*
- *This makes two "cool" drinks.*

Quick Sips

Here's a drink that comes with its own glass! Roll an orange around on the table for a few minutes. Cut off the top and stick in a straw. It's the perfect drink for kids who are on the go.

Brew a big mug of hot chocolate and add a peppermint stick for flavor.

Food Favorites

Here are a few of my favorite snacks:

_____

_____

_____

_____

_____

_____

_____

_____

TIME FOR BED!

Most children hate to hear these words — especially from a baby-sitter. Here are seven steps you can follow to make the job easier.

1. Make sure the child knows what time he must go to bed. Warn him that bedtime is approaching and stick to that time.
2. Start off by telling the child that you'd like him to get into his pajamas — but he doesn't have to go to bed yet.
3. When the time to go to bed finally arrives, go with the child and offer to talk or to read a story. If you're very lucky, the child just might fall asleep while you're reading!
4. Your job's not over yet. More than likely the child will get out of bed and join you in the living room. You have no choice but to lead him back to bed again.
5. Children are very good at finding excuses to get out of bed. They're hot, they're cold, they're thirsty, they're hungry. If the child really has a problem, take care of it. Then immediately return him to bed. Tell him firmly that he must go to sleep.
6. Sooner or later the child will fall asleep. Now you can sit back and relax. But don't get too

comfortable. Be sure to check on the sleeping child every 15 to 20 minutes to make sure everything's all right.

7. Keep the volume on the TV or radio down low. The last thing you want to do is wake up the child. Then you'll have to go back to step one and start all over again!

PEACE AND QUIET

Once the children are in bed and asleep, you'll probably have a lot of quiet time on your hands. Here are a few ideas to help make the time fly by.

The first thing you must do is **clean up** any mess you and the children have made. Be sure to put all the toys and books away. You are not expected to clean the house, but it would be a good business practice to do a little extra, such as straightening out the kitchen. It makes people want to have you come back.

Even TV can get boring, especially when none of your favorite shows are on. To add a little excitement to a dull show, why not have a guess-a-thon? Before the show starts, pick a number and a category. You might guess that the show will have five car chases or ten kisses. Then watch the show and see how close you came to guessing the correct number.

Quiet time is also a good time to get your **homework** done.

My favorite quiet time activity is: _____

_____

_____

_____

Suggested Reading

If you really want the time to fly by, bring a good book to read. Here are just a few suggestions that are guaranteed to make the minutes tick away:

The Baby-Sitters Club series by Ann M. Martin
The Dollhouse Murders by Betty Ren Wright
Junior High Jitters by M.L. Kennedy
Tom Sawyer by Mark Twain
Charlotte's Web by E.B. White
The Secret Garden by Frances Hodgson Burnett
Nothing's Fair in Fifth Grade by Barthe DeClements

You can find these books in your local bookstore or library.

EMERGENCY! EMERGENCY!

When you're working with young children, anything could go wrong. The most important thing is not to panic. Stay calm, look over the situation, and keep the list of important phone numbers close at hand. Here are some situations that might occur and a few suggestions on how to handle them.

Nightmares

Nightmares can be pretty scary, especially to a small child. If you hear a child cry out in his sleep, wake him up gently, and explain that his nightmare was just a dream. Let the child talk about the dream if he wants to, then do your best to take his mind off the nightmare and on to something more pleasant. Read him a story or find a favorite cuddly toy. Stay with the child until he's fallen back to sleep.

Injuries

It doesn't matter how careful you are, the child you're sitting for might get hurt. First check and see how serious the injury is. If the child stops crying in a few minutes and goes back to what he was doing before, it's probably not a serious injury. But if after a while the child is still crying hard or holding the injured area in a peculiar way, call for help.

Visitors

As soon as the parents leave, lock the door securely. If anyone should come to the door after they've gone, don't let him in, no matter what the person says. The only exception would be if the child's parents told you that someone was coming. Just make sure the person at the door is who he says he is. But in most cases, no one will be expected, so don't let anyone in. It is much better to be safe than sorry.

Fights

Brothers and sisters argue all the time, and they are not going to stop because you are there. The best thing to do during an argument is to ignore it — as long as no one gets hurt! One thing you can do is separate the children and get each one involved in different activities. Before long, the fighting will stop and everything will calm down.

GETTING DOWN TO BUSINESS

Now that you know everything you need to know to start baby-sitting, it's time to do the paperwork! A *good* baby-sitter keeps records of each family — what the kids like to do, if anyone's allergic to anything, what the rules of a particular house are, and anything else you think might be helpful the next time you baby-sit. Use the rest of *The Baby-sitters Club Notebook* as your diary and you'll always be prepared!

FOR THE RECORD

Family name: _____

Address: _____

Telephone: _____

Kids' Names: _____

_____

_____

Important Telephone Numbers

Nearby friend: _____

Relative: _____

Police Department: _____

Fire Department: _____

Poison Control Center: _____

Hospital: _____

Other: _____

_____

_____

BABY-SITTING DIARY

Day: _____

Date: _____

Time: _____

Notes: _____

_____

_____

_____

_____

Day: _____

Date: _____

Time: _____

Notes: _____

_____

_____

_____

_____

BABY-SITTING DIARY

Day: _____

Date: _____

Time: _____

Notes: _____

_____

_____

_____

_____

Day: _____

Date: _____

Time: _____

Notes: _____

_____

_____

_____

_____

BABY-SITTING DIARY

Day: _____

Date: _____

Time: _____

Notes: _____

_____

_____

_____

_____

Day: _____

Date: _____

Time: _____

Notes: _____

_____

_____

_____

_____

BABY-SITTING DIARY

Day: _____

Date: _____

Time: _____

Notes: _____

_____

_____

_____

_____

Day: _____

Date: _____

Time: _____

Notes: _____

_____

_____

_____

_____

BABY-SITTING DIARY

Day: _____

Date: _____

Time: _____

Notes: _____

_____

_____

_____

_____

_____

Day: _____

Date: _____

Time: _____

Notes: _____

_____

_____

_____

_____

FOR THE RECORD

Family name: _____

Address: _____

Telephone: _____

Kids' Names: _____

_____

_____

Important Telephone Numbers

Nearby friend: _____

Relative: _____

Police Department: _____

Fire Department: _____

Poison Control Center: _____

Hospital: _____

Other: _____

_____

_____

BABY-SITTING DIARY

Day: _____

Date: _____

Time: _____

Notes: _____

_____

_____

_____

_____

Day: _____

Date: _____

Time: _____

Notes: _____

_____

_____

_____

_____

BABY-SITTING DIARY

Day: _____

Date: _____

Time: _____

Notes: _____

_____

_____

_____

_____

_____

Day: _____

Date: _____

Time: _____

Notes: _____

_____

_____

_____

_____

BABY-SITTING DIARY

Day: _____

Date: _____

Time: _____

Notes: _____

_____

_____

_____

_____

_____

Day: _____

Date: _____

Time: _____

Notes: _____

_____

_____

_____

_____

BABY-SITTING DIARY

Day: _____

Date: _____

Time: _____

Notes: _____

_____

_____

_____

_____

Day: _____

Date: _____

Time: _____

Notes: _____

_____

_____

_____

_____

FOR THE RECORD

Family name: _____

Address: _____

Telephone: _____

Kids' Names: _____

_____

_____

Important Telephone Numbers

Nearby friend: _____

Relative: _____

Police Department: _____

Fire Department: _____

Poison Control Center: _____

Hospital: _____

Other: _____

_____

_____

BABY-SITTING DIARY

Day: _____

Date: _____

Time: _____

Notes: _____

_____

_____

_____

_____

Day: _____

Date: _____

Time: _____

Notes: _____

_____

_____

_____

_____

BABY-SITTING DIARY

Day: _____

Date: _____

Time: _____

Notes: _____

_____

_____

_____

_____

_____

Day: _____

Date: _____

Time: _____

Notes: _____

_____

_____

_____

_____

BABY-SITTING DIARY

Day: _____

Date: _____

Time: _____

Notes: _____

_____

_____

_____

_____

Day: _____

Date: _____

Time: _____

Notes: _____

_____

_____

_____

_____

BABY-SITTING DIARY

Day: _____

Date: _____

Time: _____

Notes: _____

_____

_____

_____

_____

Day: _____

Date: _____

Time: _____

Notes: _____

_____

_____

_____

_____

FOR THE RECORD

Family name: _____

Address: _____

Telephone: _____

Kids' Names: _____

_____

_____

Important Telephone Numbers

Nearby friend: _____

Relative: _____

Police Department: _____

Fire Department: _____

Poison Control Center: _____

Hospital: _____

Other: _____

_____

_____

BABY-SITTING DIARY

Day: _____

Date: _____

Time: _____

Notes: _____

_____

_____

_____

_____

_____

Day: _____

Date: _____

Time: _____

Notes: _____

_____

_____

_____

_____

BABY-SITTING DIARY

Day: _____

Date: _____

Time: _____

Notes: _____

_____

_____

_____

_____

Day: _____

Date: _____

Time: _____

Notes: _____

_____

_____

_____

_____

BABY-SITTING DIARY

Day: _____

Date: _____

Time: _____

Notes: _____

_____

_____

_____

_____

Day: _____

Date: _____

Time: _____

Notes: _____

_____

_____

_____

_____

BABY-SITTING DIARY

Day: _____

Date: _____

Time: _____

Notes: _____

_____

_____

_____

_____

Day: _____

Date: _____

Time: _____

Notes: _____

_____

_____

_____

_____

FOR THE RECORD

Family name: _____

Address: _____

Telephone: _____

Kids' Names: _____

_____

_____

Important Telephone Numbers

Nearby friend: _____

Relative: _____

Police Department: _____

Fire Department: _____

Poison Control Center: _____

Hospital: _____

Other: _____

_____

_____

BABY-SITTING DIARY

Day: _____

Date: _____

Time: _____

Notes: _____

_____

_____

_____

_____

Day: _____

Date: _____

Time: _____

Notes: _____

_____

_____

_____

_____

BABY-SITTING DIARY

Day: _____

Date: _____

Time: _____

Notes: _____

_____

_____

_____

_____

Day: _____

Date: _____

Time: _____

Notes: _____

_____

_____

_____

_____

BABY-SITTING DIARY

Day: _____

Date: _____

Time: _____

Notes: _____

_____

_____

_____

_____

Day: _____

Date: _____

Time: _____

Notes: _____

_____

_____

_____

_____

BABY-SITTING DIARY

Day: _____

Date: _____

Time: _____

Notes: _____

_____

_____

_____

_____

_____

Day: _____

Date: _____

Time: _____

Notes: _____

_____

_____

_____

_____

FOR THE RECORD

Family name: _____

Address: _____

Telephone: _____

Kids' Names: _____

_____

_____

Important Telephone Numbers

Nearby friend: _____

Relative: _____

Police Department: _____

Fire Department: _____

Poison Control Center: _____

Hospital: _____

Other: _____

_____

_____

BABY-SITTING DIARY

Day: _____

Date: _____

Time: _____

Notes: _____

_____

_____

_____

_____

Day: _____

Date: _____

Time: _____

Notes: _____

_____

_____

_____

_____

BABY-SITTING DIARY

Day: _____

Date: _____

Time: _____

Notes: _____

_____

_____

_____

_____

Day: _____

Date: _____

Time: _____

Notes: _____

_____

_____

_____

_____

BABY-SITTING DIARY

Day: _____

Date: _____

Time: _____

Notes: _____

_____

_____

_____

_____

Day: _____

Date: _____

Time: _____

Notes: _____

_____

_____

_____

_____

BABY-SITTING DIARY

Day: _____

Date: _____

Time: _____

Notes: _____

_____

_____

_____

_____

Day: _____

Date: _____

Time: _____

Notes: _____

_____

_____

_____

_____

Total hours spent baby-sitting

_____

_____

_____

_____

_____

_____

_____

_____

_____

_____

_____

_____

Total money earned

_____

_____

_____

_____

_____

_____

_____

_____

_____

_____

_____

_____

Things I bought with my baby-sitting money	Things I'd like to buy with my baby-sitting money
_____	_____
_____	_____
_____	_____
_____	_____
_____	_____
_____	_____
_____	_____
_____	_____
_____	_____
_____	_____
_____	_____
_____	_____
_____	_____
_____	_____